This book belongs to

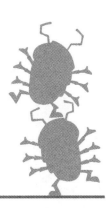

_____

Blueberries on Parade

Published by Advance Publishers
www.advance-publishers.com

Written by K. Emily Hutta and Victoria Saxon
Illustrated by Dean Kleven, Adam Devaney, and Yakovetic
Editorial development and management by Bumpy Slide Books
Illustrations produced by Disney Publishing Creative Development
Cover design by Deborah Boone

ISBN: 1-57973-018-3

"Our troop salutes you, Francis," said the leader of the Blueberries. All the girls smiled their biggest smiles.

Francis the ladybug sat in his bed in the ant infirmary. He had rescued Princess Dot, the smallest

Blueberry, from a bird. That's how he had hurt
his leg.

"And to honor you, we've added spots to our
bandannas," said Teeny.

"And guess what else?" exclaimed Dot. "We want
you to be our honorary Blueberry troop den mother!"
Francis scowled. Dot and the other Blueberries
thought Francis was a female because he was a *lady*bug.

"Wait a second!" cried Francis.

Just then Dr. Flora came in. "Okay. Let's run along, girls. The patient needs to rest. You can visit again later on."

A few days later, Dot and two of the
Blueberries returned to Francis's room for
a meeting. They were very excited as they
giggled and talked to one another.

11

Francis sighed. "What do I know about being a den mother?" he grumbled. "How did I get stuck with this job?"

Dot raised her hand. "May I start the meeting?" she asked. "I have something important to say."

"Yeah, all right," muttered Francis.

"We have another big surprise for you, Den Mother," began Dot. "To thank you and the other circus bugs for all that you've done, we are going to put together the best parade ever!"

"And we want *you* to help us," Teeny added. "Right, girls?"

"Right!" answered the other Blueberries enthusiastically.

"Oh, great," thought Francis.

"Well, girls," he said, "why don't you go outside and get started? I'll just take a little rest and join you later, okay?"

"Okay!" the Blueberries cheered. Then they rushed over to Francis to give him a hug. "Watch out for my leg!" Francis cried.

But it was too late. The girls were already piling onto his cast.

"Oops! Sorry, Den Mother," said Dot. She and the other Blueberries tried to make Francis comfortable again.

"We've never held a parade before," Dot said. "What do we do first?"

Francis tried hard to be patient. "Why don't you start by making a nice little flag for the parade? *Outside!*"

"Hey, yeah!" exclaimed Dot. "Thanks for the great idea!"

The next day, the Blueberries met and happily made plans for the first-ever Blueberry parade. They decided they would march from the Blueberry clubhouse to the banquet hall. There, the parade would end with a big party.

But the hardest part would be making the flag. They wanted to make it extra special to please Francis. But none of the designs they came up with seemed quite right.

"I know!" Dot suggested finally. "Let's each make our own special decoration to put on the flag."

The other Blueberries loved the idea. Soon they were sticking bright bits of flower petals, pebbles, and leaves on the flag with tree sap.

When they were finished, the flag looked wonderful! The Blueberries were just getting ready to show the flag to Francis when they heard a *SPLAT!* The flag had been hit by a chunk of berry!

"What's happening?" cried Dot.

SPLAT! Another glob of juice hit the flag. The Blueberries scrambled to save their flag, but it was too late. There was bright red juice all over it.

Suddenly the girls heard laughing. They turned to see the Boysenberry troop grinning at them.

"Those mean boys!" exclaimed Teeny. "They always ruin everything. Now what are we going to do?"

"Let's go ask our den mother!" Dot suggested. "Francis will help us!"

A little while later, the Blueberries stood sadly around Francis's bed. They were holding their stained flag.

"The Boysenberries did it!" Dot sobbed.

She looked so upset, Francis couldn't help but feel sorry for her.

"Poor girls," he thought. "Maybe I can help them out a little."

"Okay, Blueberries!" Francis exclaimed. "You want to keep those Boysenberries out of your antennae?"

"Yeah!" cried the Blueberries.

"Then listen to your den mother!" Francis commanded. "If we all work together, we can still have the parade—and teach those Boysenberries a lesson!"

Over the next several weeks, the Blueberries met
with Francis. He helped them make a new flag. He
also told them they needed to get ready in case the
Boysenberries attacked again.

"The key is to outsmart them," Francis told the
girls. "And I think I know how."
Then he told them all about his plan.

On the day of the parade, Francis was
finally able to get out of bed. After wishing
the Blueberries good luck, he went to join the
other circus bugs to wait for the parade to begin.

But the Boysenberries were ready, too. They
had put berry juice along the parade path so the
Blueberries would slip in it. The boys hid nearby
waiting for the parade to pass by.

Suddenly the Boysenberries heard the sounds of the parade. But it wasn't anywhere near them!

"Hey!" cried one of the boys. "What's going on?"

The Boysenberries ran out into the road. They slipped and slid in their own berry juice! They had been tricked! The Blueberries had chosen another route.

Meanwhile, the Blueberries had begun marching along the other side of a nearby hill. The Boysenberries would not be able to ruin their flag this time!

Francis sat proudly among the circus bugs and watched the parade approach.

"Look at that flag!" he declared to his friends. "Isn't it great?"

The Blueberries stopped in front of Francis and saluted him.

"Well done, girls," Francis said.

The Blueberries cheered. Francis smiled and shook his head. Those little Blueberries sure had grown on him. "Maybe being a den mother isn't so bad after all!" he thought.

Dear Blueberry Journal,

Poor Francis. Everybody figures that since he's called a ladybug, he's a lady. You know—a girl. A female. Like me. But he's not.

I told Francis he should just start telling people he's a beetle (which he is). But he said that ladybugs are not your average beetles. It seems there are thousands of different kinds of ladybugs, and they come in lots of different colors and patterns. Francis even met a ladybug with stripes once!

Francis is proud to be a ladybug. He'd just rather be called a "gentlemanbug" instead!

Till next time,
Dot

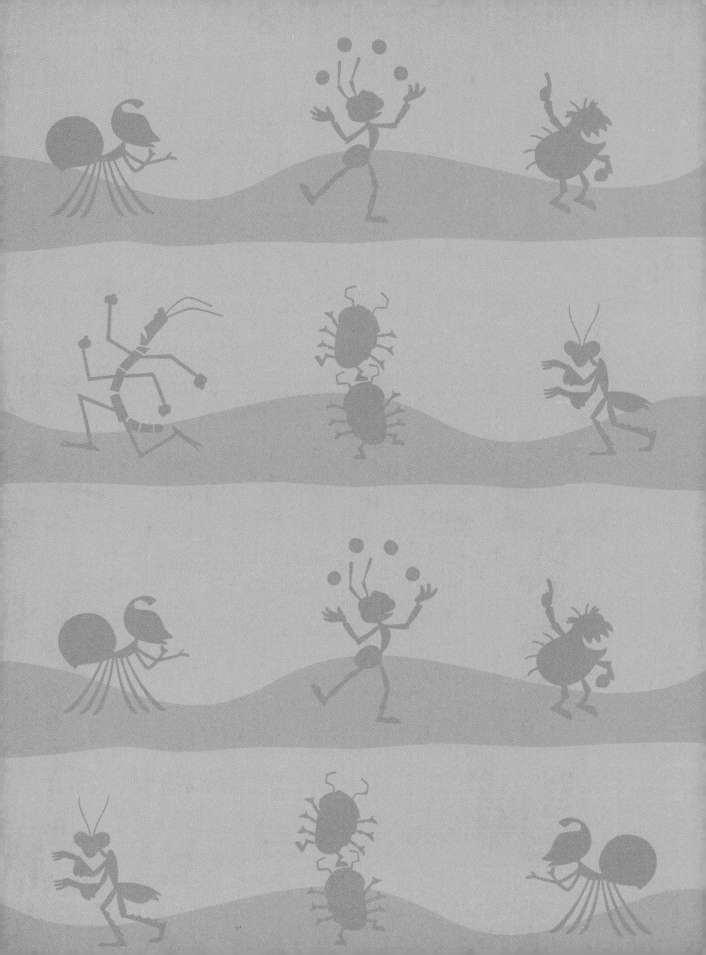